David M

 W9-CFS-234

STEVEN SPIELBERG PRESENTS

A Dinosaur's Story

THE MOVIE STORYBOOK

Adapted by Justine Korman
From a screenplay by John Patrick Shanley
Based on the book by Hudson Talbott
Illustrated by Beverly Lazor-Bahr

TM & © 1993 by Universal City Studios, Inc. & Amblin Entertainment, Inc. All rights reserved. WE'RE BACK! A DINOSAUR'S STORY and the WE'RE BACK! A DINOSAUR'S STORY logo are trademarks of Universal City Studios, Inc. & Amblin Entertainment, Inc. Published by Grosset & Dunlap, Inc., a member of The Putnam & Grosset Group, New York. Published simultaneously in Canada. Printed in the U.S.A. Library of Congress Catalog Card Number: 93-70451 ISBN 0-448-40444-3   A B C D E F G H I J

Grosset & Dunlap • New York

On a bright spring morning, Mother Bird brought a juicy worm back to the nest. Buster, the youngest, headed straight for it, but his greedy brothers snatched it away. Poor Buster was shoved right out of the nest!

"Whoa there, little fella!" said a friendly Tyrannosaurus named Rex. "Where'd you fall from?"

"Noplace!" chirped the little bluebird.

"Noplace? I've never been there. Don't you have a mom somewhere who's probably worried about you?" Rex asked.

"No. I'm an orphan," Buster lied. He was sick and tired of being shoved around at home. "I'm gonna run away and join the circus!" he said.

"You know, I knew a little fella who ran away and joined the circus," Rex remembered. Rex knew a lot of things. He was one smart dinosaur. But he hadn't always been smart.

"This was a long time ago," Rex began. "A very long time ago...."

Back then, Rex was a real terror. He was stupid and violent, and hungry all the time. He devoured any prehistoric creature he could find.

One day Rex was just about to gulp down a shivering snack, when he heard a strange beeping sound. He looked around, but didn't see anything. And when he opened his jaws to gulp down his lunch, he realized that his main course had escaped! Rex was fuming, and that beeping was driving him crazy! Then, suddenly, he saw something shiny hovering over his head.

It was a spaceship! When it landed, a weird little creature popped out. He set up a display of cereal boxes and signs that said: BRAIN GRAIN CEREAL, THE I.Q. ENHANCER, and WHY BE STUPID WHEN YOU CAN EAT BRAIN GRAIN?

"Hey, kiddo, my name is Vorb, and this is your lucky day!" the creature jabbered. "Take one bite of Brain Grain Cereal and you'll be smart." Rex just stood there. "Can't make up your mind? Or don't you have one?" Vorb asked.

Rex opened his massive jaws and roared. Vorb dove into the spaceship, but Rex jammed his head right in after him. In a panic, Vorb poured cereal down Rex's throat. Rex roared, and groaned, and…crooned. "Rrrrrow, row, row your boat…Hey, who turned on the lights? I'm talking!"

"Hiyiyi! It only took 280 servings of Brain Grain to jump start your skull," Vorb exclaimed. "How 'bout some lunch?"

"What's lunch?" wondered Rex, squeezing into the spaceship.

Vorb gave Rex a name tag and introduced him to the other dinosaurs who were having a feast of hot dogs, popcorn, cotton candy, and orange soda.

An attractive Pterodactyl introduced herself. "I'm Elsa," she cooed, fluttering her wings.

"I'm Woog," said a Triceratops. "You wanna hot dog?"

Rex tried one, and liked it. "Now that's what I call lunch!"

"That's what you used to call me," joked Dweeb. "But let's face it, we've evolved."

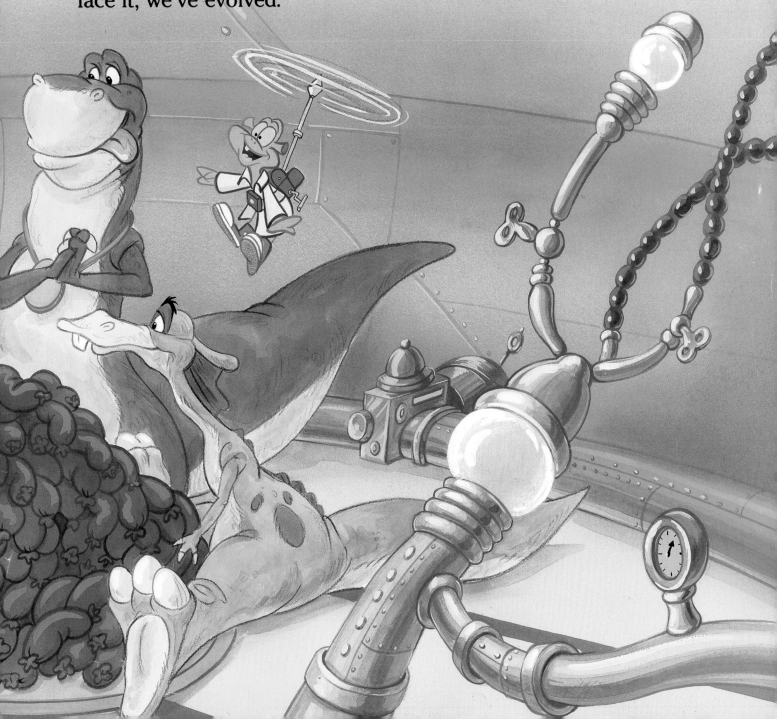

While the dinosaurs gobbled heaps of hot dogs, the spaceship captain greeted them. "Welcome, friends. I am Captain Neweyes, the inventor of Brain Grain Cereal. I come from the Far Future, where I listen to wishes on my Wish Radio and do my best to make them come true."

The captain tuned the radio into the Middle Future. A babble of children's voices wished for many things, like a million dollars or to fly like a bird. But most of all, the children wished they could see real dinosaurs.

"Son of a gunosaur! That's us!" Woog cried.

"Lots of children want to meet you," Captain Neweyes said. "What do you say?"

"We'll do it!" Rex declared.

Just then the bottom of the ship opened and the dinosaurs saw the lights of New York City twinkling below. "It's a world covered with jewels!" Elsa gasped.

While Vorb handed out parachutes, Captain Neweyes told the dinosaurs to find kindly Dr. Juliet Bleeb at the Museum of Natural History. Neweyes also warned them to stay clear of his cruel brother, Professor Screweyes. Then Vorb shoved a big rubber raft out of the spaceship and pushed out the dinosaurs one by one.

"Farewell, my friends!" Neweyes called as the dinosaurs drifted down into the dawn.

The dinosaurs splashed down in a murky river. Water rocked in huge swells, swamping a tiny raft floating nearby. Unaware of the damage they'd caused, the dinosaurs helped each other aboard their huge rubber dinghy. The sun was just rising, and its rays lit up the magnificent towers of Manhattan.

"What is it?" awestruck Elsa asked.

"It's New York City, you morons," a tiny voice snapped.

That's when Rex looked around and saw little Louie bobbing in the waves.

"Help me!" the angry boy demanded. "What're you, stupid?"

Rex scooped Louie out of the water and held him on his palm. "What're you guys supposed to be, anyway?" the boy asked.

"Dinosaurs, actually," Elsa informed him.

"You do got that look," Louie admitted. "I mean you're big."

"Well, you're very small," Elsa said.

"I'm big enough to suit my own purposes," Louie declared.

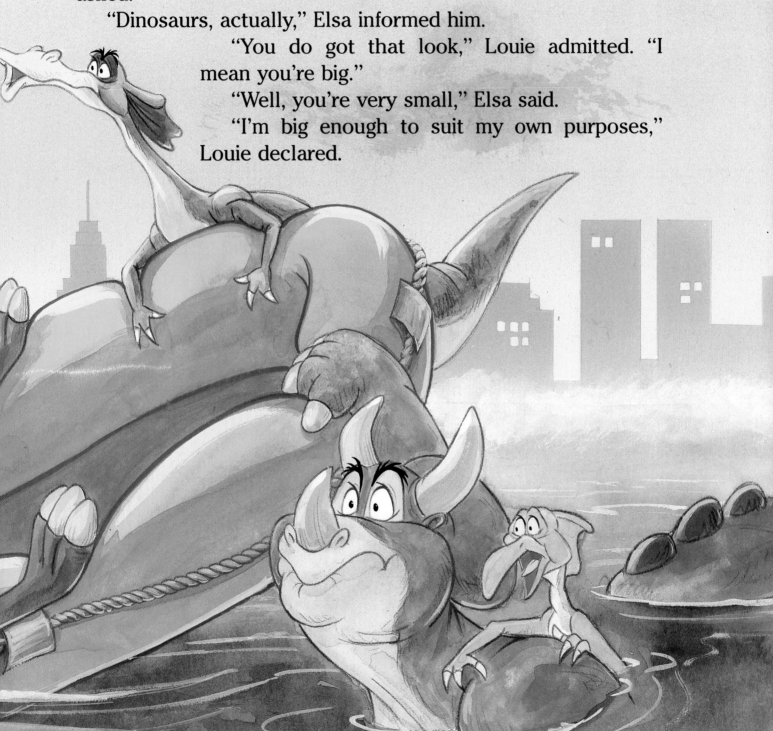

"You wanna know somethin'?" the boy continued. "All my life I dreamed of building a little raft, sailing across New York Harbor, and joining the circus. I'm finally sailing along and you clowns drop out of the blue and wreck the whole kit and caboodle."

"Sorry about that," Woog said as the dinghy reached the dock.

"Sorry don't cut it," Louie sneered. "This is a tough town in a tough world and you gotta have your fists up to get by."

"That's what I thought before I could think," Rex said. "Your attitude is prehistoric. Now that we're smart, my friends and I know violence doesn't solve anything. But we're sorry about your raft and we'd like to help you get to the circus."

Louie knew the circus was way uptown in Central Park. "How are we all gonna get there?" he wondered. Then he looked at Elsa and got an idea. "Hey, bat, can you fly?" he asked her.

"I'm not a bat!" Elsa answered huffily. "But of *course* I can fly." Louie climbed on her neck and off they flew, soaring over the city.

On a street far below, crowds and floats gathered for the start of the city's grand Thanksgiving Day Parade.

"Bingo! That's our ticket uptown!" Louie exclaimed.

On the way back to tell the others his plan, Louie spotted a pretty girl crying on a balcony of a fancy building. When Elsa landed on the ledge, the girl looked frightened.

"Hey, don't panic. I'm a good guy. My name is Louie," Louie said. "Why are you crying?"

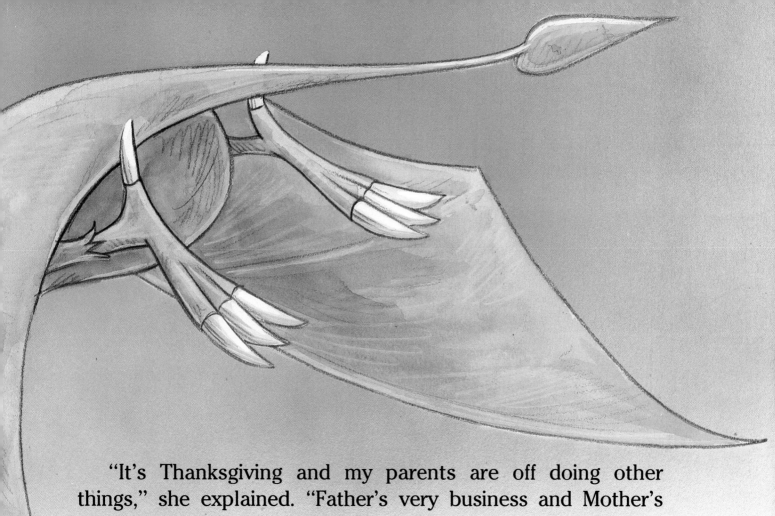

"It's Thanksgiving and my parents are off doing other things," she explained. "Father's very business and Mother's very social." The girl smiled. "My name is Cecilia Nuthatch."

Louie said, "Well, Cecilia, my parents got a lotta kids and I been lost in the shuffle. So I'm running away to the circus. What do you say you come fly with me?"

"Mmm, well…all right, I will!" Cecilia said.

When Louie, Cecilia, and Elsa met up with the dinosaurs again, Louie introduced everyone to Cecilia. Then he got down to business.

"Here's the plan," he said. "You guys can pretend to be floats in the Thanksgiving Day Parade. That way, nobody will know you're real." Then Louie asked, "Where are you guys goin' after you drop us off at the circus?"

"To the Museum of Natural History," Rex replied.

"Perfect," Louie said. "That's not even out of the way."

The parade was amazing! There were beautiful floats, colorful balloons, marching bands, and lots and lots of people. Dancers twirled and leaped between the rows of cheering spectators. Elsa flew among the giant balloons. Rex sang along with the rollicking marching band and kicked up his gigantic heels.

Up ahead, Rex thought he recognized a fellow dinosaur and hurried to greet it. Rex's sharp claws sank into soft rubber and KAPOW! The dinosaur balloon popped!

Suddenly, the parade turned into a whirlwind of chaos. The bands bumped into each other. Balloon strings tangled. Spectators stared at Rex and his friends. In one great gasp of panic, the confused crowd realized that the dinosaurs were real.

"I think things just took a turn for the worst," Louie sighed.

Police arrived in cars and helicopters, sirens blaring.

"Quick, split up!" Louie shouted. "We'll meet you at the circus in Central Park. Run!"

Rex looked confused. "Central Park? Where's that?" Then he noticed a big poster on a wall: PROFESSOR SCREWEYES' ECCENTRIC CIRCUS, NOW APPEARING IN CENTRAL PARK!

"Hey," Rex said. "That's the bad guy."

Just then the police came after the dinosaurs. They took off in different directions, running for their lives. They ran up and down and around the streets of New York.

Finally, they all met up in an empty building.

"Whew, that was close," said Woog.

"No kidding," Rex agreed. "But we're safe now."

Suddenly there was a huge explosion and the dinosaurs found themselves soaring through the air. With a series of thumps, they landed in Central Park.

At that very moment, the children climbed out of a cab in another part of the park. They followed a gloomy path that twisted among the trees. Savage dogs barked at them from the ends of straining chains. A cat hissed. A poster pasted on a garbage can read: PROFESSOR SCREWEYES' ECCENTRIC CIRCUS. KEEP COMING, OR MAYBE YOU SHOULD STOP RIGHT HERE.

Louie looked around the creepy path.

"Maybe we should go back," Cecilia whispered. But just then they noticed peculiar people in dark clothes swarming out of a big black circus tent. "We're already here," Louie said.

Louie and Cecilia peeked inside the dismal tent. In the center ring a very funny clown pranced and danced for a strange, dark man on a stool. Whenever the man snapped his fingers, the clown did a new trick, each one wackier than the one before.

Cecilia couldn't help laughing at the clown. When the man on the stool heard her giggle, he slowly turned and stared at the children with mismatched eyes, one blue-black and the other a sharp, shiny steel screw. Professor Screweyes' voice was cold. "Who laughed?!"

"I did," Louie said bravely.

"No, it was me, sir," Cecilia admitted.

Screweyes dismissed the clown. "Stubbs, get out of here." Then he addressed Louie and Cecilia. "You missed the show, kids. Come back tomorrow."

Louie explained that they hadn't come to see the circus but to join it.

"I'll take you on if you want," Screweyes said craftily. "Standard contract." He pulled out a blank piece of paper with a wax seal. Then he pricked Louie's finger and pressed it against the blank page. The paper filled magically with writing, and Louie's signature appeared at the bottom!

Determined to stand by Louie, Cecilia pricked her own finger and pressed it on the contract.

Cecilia's signature appeared beneath Louie's.

No sooner had they sealed their fate than they heard Rex's voice from outside the tent. "Louie, where are you?"

"Who is that?" Screweyes asked.

"My friend Rex," Louie said, and he led the professor out into the moonlight, where all the dinosaurs were waiting.

Rex took one look at the stranger and cried, "That's Professor Screweyes! His brother warned us about him."

"So he's fed you that Brain Grain stuff!" Screweyes concluded. "Did he show you that hokey Wish Radio? I have a radio, too. Care to see it?"

"No way," Rex said. "We don't want anything to do with you. Come on, kids. Let's go to the museum."

"They're not going anywhere!" declared Screweyes as he whipped out the contract. "They're under contract to me! For a very long time!"

Cecilia started to cry, and Louie tried to comfort her. "It's gonna be all right," he said.

Screweyes smiled cruelly. "Only if we can work out something with your friends."

Everyone followed the professor to his radio. "This is a time of loud wishes, but even louder fears," Screweyes told them. "I find out what people are scared of and that's what I give them in my circus— whether it's snakes or fire or rats or spiders."

"This station comes in loudest of all!" Screweyes turned the Fright Radio's dial. "Do you hear what they're most afraid of, my friends? Monsters! YOU—with a little help."

The professor held up a vial of glowing green pills. "Brain Drain! The antidote to my brother's goody-two-shoes cereal. This will take you back and make you mindless monsters."

"We're not going to take anything. We'll just say no," Rex refused.

"I can't stop you," Screweyes said. "But the kids are mine!" Then he fixed his spinning hypnotic eye on Cecilia and Louie.

Under his spell the children were powerless to resist taking the Brain Drain pills. "This is just a temporary dose," Screweyes said. "By way of demonstration."

Cecilia and Louie instantly became half-human and half-monkey, chattering insanely.

Rex growled. "Change them back or I'll..."

"Or you'll what?" Screweyes asked coolly. He knew Rex was no longer savage enough to carry out his threat. Instead, Screweyes made an offer. "If you take the Brain Drain, the kids go free. If not, they're my new sideshow—the Wild Children of Calcazar."

The dinosaurs wanted to help, but felt afraid.

"I'll take it," Rex said at last. Woog, Dweeb, and Elsa agreed to take the pills too.

"Good!" Screweyes smirked. "Now come with me and be wild again."

"Whatever happens, happens to us all," Rex said bravely. The dinosaurs followed the professor into the tent, leaving Louie and Cecilia alone.

Before long, the pills wore off and the kids became themselves again. Louie and Cecilia were so exhausted by their strange ordeal that they fell asleep.

While Louie and Cecilia snoozed, Screweyes fastened chains on the dinosaurs and locked them in a row of giant cages inside the circus tent. Hundreds of cawing ebony crows swarmed inside the billowing black canvas.

"What I wouldn't give for a hot dog," Woog said sadly.

"With just everything on it," Elsa sighed wistfully.

"The bun. I like the bun," Dweeb mourned.

Meanwhile Screweyes stood nearby, loading a pill gun with the glowing Brain Drain pills.

As he worked, Screweyes told the dinosaurs why he surrounded himself with crows. "When I was a little boy, I was scared out of my wits by a flock of crows flapping all around me. Ever since I've been terrified of the black birds. But I keep them by me so I can be their master. I am the Master of my Fear!"

"This guy is nuts," Rex muttered under his breath.

Screweyes aimed the gun. "Open your mouths."

"First destroy the children's contract," Rex protested.

"Oh, all right," Screweyes said, and he burned the contract. Then, laughing madly, the professor walked down the line of cages, firing Brain Drain pills into the mouth of each dinosaur.

Soon Rex and the others were roaring like wild beasts.

"That's right. Give in to that rage. Be senseless, bloodthirsty monsters. You'll terrify my grateful audience!" Professor Screweyes gloated.

At sunrise, Louie and Cecilia awoke, bathed in light. They weren't sure where they were until Stubbs said, "Good morning." The clown held a tray of breakfast for two.

"Louie! It's that funny clown," Cecilia said.

"So you really thought I was funny?" the clown asked eagerly. "I can never make the professor laugh. Lately the show's gotten scary. I like comedy, myself. The professor promised he'll put my routine in the show if I can make him laugh. I just haven't been able to bring it off yet, that's all."

While the children ate their pancakes, Stubbs showed them one of his funniest routines. The children clapped and laughed. Stubbs was stunned. "The professor didn't laugh at all."

"The guy's crazy!" Louie said.

"Not really," Stubbs replied, defending his boss. "Look, he told me you gotta get out of here after breakfast. He tore up your contract."

"But what about the dinosaurs?" asked Louie.

"Forget them and go about your merry," Stubbs told them.

But Louie would not leave until he saw his friends again.

In the tent full of cages and crows, the dinosaurs roared and rampaged. They slammed against the bars, clawing at the children and the clown when they came near.

"What happened to them, Mr. Stubbs?" Cecilia asked.

"They made a deal with the professor. They took this stuff that sent 'em off the deep end so he'd tear up your contract," the clown explained.

"You mean they're like this because of us?!" Louie cried.

Stubbs nodded. "Your friends are starring in tonight's show."

"You've gotta get us into that show! It's the only way we can get near enough to rescue Rex and the others," Louie said. Then he grabbed Stubbs' suspenders. "Wake up, Stubbs! Screweyes will never laugh at you until he's fed you full of those pills and you're gibberin' like a maniac baboon."

"All right, I'll get you in," Stubbs finally agreed. "Not 'cause of what you said. But because you laughed at my jokes."

At twilight, two hooded men blew twisted trumpets before the entrance to the black tent. The dark flaps opened and the gloomy crowd trudged past three shrieking, grimacing goblins. Under their ghoulish disguises the goblins were really Stubbs, Louie, and Cecilia.

"I don't understand these people," Cecilia whispered.

"Don't you see? They come to get scared," Stubbs told her. "The show's starting. Let's get in our places for the opening."

A spotlight struck the glittering costume of the wicked ringmaster. The professor's voice boomed hypnotically under the big top. "Ladies and gentlemen. Welcome to the most terrifying show on earth: Professor Screweyes' Eccentric Circus. We will shock you! We will scare you witless! Without further ado, I give you the Grand Infernal Parade!"

Screweyes fired a flare pistol and the barbaric band struck up a fiendish fanfare for the Grand Entry of slobbering jackals, hysterical hyenas, and mad elephants. Witches shrieked. Cavemen swung knobby clubs. Black horses pulled floats full of gargoyles and goblins, including Louie, Cecilia, and Stubbs.

"Just look scary and wave your pitchforks," Stubbs said.

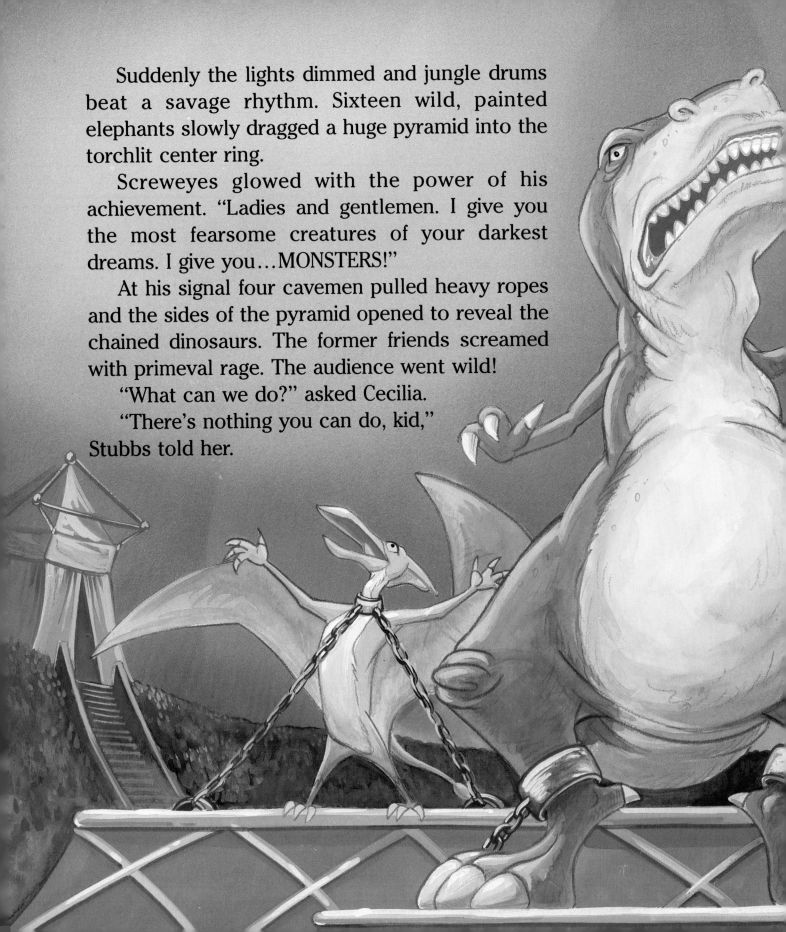

Suddenly the lights dimmed and jungle drums beat a savage rhythm. Sixteen wild, painted elephants slowly dragged a huge pyramid into the torchlit center ring.

Screweyes glowed with the power of his achievement. "Ladies and gentlemen. I give you the most fearsome creatures of your darkest dreams. I give you…MONSTERS!"

At his signal four cavemen pulled heavy ropes and the sides of the pyramid opened to reveal the chained dinosaurs. The former friends screamed with primeval rage. The audience went wild!

"What can we do?" asked Cecilia.

"There's nothing you can do, kid," Stubbs told her.

Screweyes focused his pinwheel eye on Rex. "Now I will attempt to master the most fearsome of all dinosaurs—the mighty Tyrannosaurus rex! Look in my eye, you bloodthirsty thing!"

Rex clawed and roared, but the professor's eye cast its evil spell. And Rex became obedient.

"Remove his shackles," Screweyes commanded. Then he ordered Rex to take two giant steps. Rex lurched toward the audience and the crowd shrieked with terror.

"So you see! The creature that scares you all does not scare me!" Screweyes boasted. "I am the Master of Fear!"

As Screweyes spoke, one of the black crows started pecking at a control box marked DON'T TOUCH. Suddenly there were fireworks going off all around Rex, waking him up. No longer a senseless slave, Rex seized Screweyes in his powerful claws.

"He's gonna eat the professor!" Stubbs screamed.

"Oh, please," wished Cecilia. "Please let no bad happen."

Realizing that Rex had to be stopped, Louie bolted from his hiding place and rushed to his dinosaur friend.

"Don't do it!" Louie shouted. "Don't be like them! Don't ruin everything 'cause you're mad or scared. I know I act tough, but that's 'cause I'm scared. Don't be just another bully spoiling the way the world could be! Rex means king. Be a king, Rex."

Somehow, despite the Brain Drain, Rex heard Louie's words and he dropped Screweyes on the sawdust-covered floor. Louie hugged Rex's giant leg and the dinosaur smiled down at him.

Suddenly the tent top burst into flames and Neweyes' spaceship glided down. Lasers cut the dinosaurs' shackles as a mechanical arm poured Brain Grain into their mouths.

Soon the dinosaurs' roars turned into a rousing round of "Row, row, row your boat."

Captain Neweyes stepped from the spaceship. His evil brother lay at his feet. "I should have known you were behind this," Screweyes fumed.

"You'd already been done in by these kids when I got here," Neweyes said. Then he turned to Cecilia. "I heard your wish on my Wish Radio. Very good!"

Dweeb was dizzy with confusion. "What happened?" he asked. "Boy, oh boy, do I have a headache."

"All aboard!" Neweyes cried. "I have a surprise for you."

"What about me?" Screweyes whined. The flock of awful crows hovered over the professor, who sprawled in the sawdust.

"I'm leaving you here," Neweyes said. "With your fears flying around you."

"I'm leaving you too," Stubbs announced proudly. "Since I can't make you laugh, it's time to get back to the real circus. Good-bye!" Stubbs walked off, whistling a happy tune. The children and the dinosaurs followed Captain Neweyes into the gleaming spaceship.

Before long the dinosaurs arrived at the Museum of Natural History. Dr. Juliet Bleeb met them at the big double doors.

"Welcome, welcome. You took so long, I almost gave up. I'm very pleased to meet you," she said cheerily.

Dr. Bleeb had prepared a banquet with hot dogs and popcorn and fruit and french fries and orange soda. After their adventure, everyone was very hungry. Woog shouted joyously, "Chow time, everybody!"

"How good of you to have us," Neweyes said politely.

"Delightful! A dream come true." Dr. Bleeb beamed.

The next day still more dreams came true. Over the entrance to the Museum of Natural History a colorful banner announced:

While grown-ups waited outside, Dr. Bleeb ushered eager children into a special exhibit of dinosaur statues.

But once the door was tightly shut, the "statues" came to life and talked to the thrilled children.

"This will be our little secret, okay?" Rex whispered. And to this day, no grown-up knows the truth about the statues.

•   •   •

"That's what happened," Rex said to Buster Bird, who lay fast asleep on the dinosaur's long, scaly nose. "Louie and Cecilia patched things up with their folks, who were very glad to have them back home. The kids are still the best of friends. They often come to visit me and the other dinosaurs at the museum."

Rex gently lifted Buster back into his cozy nest. "And once in a while I get out to play a little golf," the genial giant concluded. Then he sighed. "Good night, little tough guy. Remember my story."